WEEKLY **WR** READER®
EARLY LEARNING LIBRARY

How Plants Grow

How Corn Grows

by Joanne Mattern

Reading consultant: Susan Nations, M.Ed.,
author, literacy coach,
and consultant in literacy development

Please visit our web site at: www.earlyliteracy.cc
For a free color catalog describing Weekly Reader® Early Learning Library's list
of high-quality books, call 1-877-445-5824 (USA) or 1-800-387-3178 (Canada).
Weekly Reader® Early Learning Library's fax: (414) 336-0164.

Library of Congress Cataloging-in-Publication Data

Mattern, Joanne, 1963-
    How corn grows / by Joanne Mattern.
        p. cm. — (How plants grow)
    Includes bibliographical references and index.
    ISBN 0-8368-6330-5 (lib. bdg.)
    ISBN 0-8368-6337-2 (softcover)
    1. Corn—Growth—Juvenile literature. 2. Corn—Development—
Juvenile literature. I. Title.
QK495.G74M3655   2006
584'.92—dc22   2005025233

This edition first published in 2006 by
Weekly Reader® Early Learning Library
A Member of the WRC Media Family of Companies
330 West Olive Street, Suite 100
Milwaukee, WI 53212 USA

Managing editor: Valerie J. Weber
Art direction: Tammy West
Cover design and page layout: Kami Strunsee
Picture research: Cisley Celmer

Picture credits: Cover, p. 17 © David Young-Wolff/PhotoEdit; Cover background,
title, © Diane Laska-Swanke; p. 5 © Peter Pearson/Stone/Getty Images; pp. 7, 9, 21
© Michael Newman/PhotoEdit; p. 11 © Andy Sacks/ Stone/Getty Images; p. 13 ©
Nigel Cattlin/Holt Studios/Photo Researchers, Inc.; p. 15 © David R. Frazier/ Photo
Researchers, Inc.; p. 19 © Karen Kasmauski/National Geographic Society Image Collection

Printed in the United States of America

1 2 3 4 5 6 7 8 9 10 09 08 07 06

Note to Educators and Parents

Reading is such an exciting adventure for young children! They are beginning to integrate their oral language skills with written language. To encourage children along the path to early literacy, books must be colorful, engaging, and interesting; they should invite the young reader to explore both the print and the pictures.

How Plants Grow is a new series designed to introduce young readers to the life cycle of familiar plants. In simple, easy-to-read language, each book explains how a specific plant begins, grows, and changes.

Each book is specially designed to support the young reader in the reading process. The familiar topics are appealing to young children and invite them to read — and re-read — again and again. The full-color photographs and enhanced text further support the student during the reading process.

In addition to serving as wonderful picture books in schools, libraries, homes, and other places where children learn to love reading, these books are specifically intended to be read within an instructional guided reading group. This small group setting allows beginning readers to work with a fluent adult model as they make meaning from the text. After children develop fluency with the text and content, the book can be read independently. Children and adults alike will find these books supportive, engaging, and fun!

— Susan Nations, M.Ed., author, literacy coach, and consultant in literacy development

Corn starts small. Corn grows
tall. It grows from a tiny seed.

A corn seed is called a **kernel**. We plant the kernel in the ground.

kernel

Corn kernels need lots of room to grow.

9

A corn stalk sprouts from the seed. Many leaves grow from the stalk.

stalk

11

What is under all those
leaves? Ears of corn!

13

Each ear has many kernels.
Silk grows on top of each
ear, too.

silk

It is time to pick the corn!

17

We save some kernels to plant in the spring.

Now it is time to eat the corn!

Do you like corn with butter?

Glossary

kernel — a corn seed

seed — part of a plant that grows
into a new plant

silk — thin strips that grow on ears of
corn. Silk looks like hair.

sprouts — grows or springs up

stalk — the stem of a plant

For More Information

Books

Anna's Corn. Barbara Santucci (Eerdmans Books
     for Young Readers)
From Kernel to Corn. Start to Finish (series).
     Robin Nelson (Lerner Publishing)
I Like Corn. Robin Pickering (Children's Press)
Pick, Pull, Snap: Where Once a Flower Bloomed.
     Lola M. Schaeffer (Greenwillow)

Web Sites

CornCam from Iowa Farmer Today
www.iowafarmer.com/corn_cam
See photos and read updates about corn growing in
an Iowa cornfield.

The Great Corn Adventure
www.urbanext.uiuc.edu/corn
A fun video explains how corn grows and the
many ways to eat this tasty food.

Index

About the Author

Joanne Mattern has written more than 150 books for children. Her favorite things to write about are animals, nature, history, sports, and famous people. Joanne also works in her local library. She lives in New York State with her husband, three daughters, and assorted pets. She enjoys animals, music, going to baseball games, reading, and visiting schools to talk about her books.